Touch Of Death
Warrior Princess

Stacey Hunter

Platinum House
Publishing

Print Edition

ISBN-13: 978-1-68096-013-6

All persons, places and organizations in this book---except those clearly in the public domain--are fictitious, and any resemblance that may seem to exist to actual persons, places or organizations living, dead or defunct is purely coincidental. These are works of friction.

Touch Of Death
Warrior Princess

A special thank you to Peter

OTHER BOOKS BY STACEY HUNTER

Warrior Princess - Slayer's Den

ISBN-13: 978-1-68096-011-2

Warrior Princess - Battle For The Forest

SBN-13: 978-1-68096-009-9

Warrior Princess - Dangerous Grounds

ISBN-13: 978-1-68096-015-0

Touch of Death

THE GOLDEN GODDESS

******

Hunger stalked the land. Rain had forsaken the village. And the voracious Abama Warriors led by Abigale—Goddess of all the Forest. The Golden Goddess—paraded persistently against the walls of the Great Kilmer to lay to rest the prehistoric curse of Leman bin Ali.

CHAPTER ONE

*****

Abigale shook water from her long golden locks and stepped out of the swimming pool, majestic, her tanned beauty glowing bright in the sunlight.

The hot sun hugged her slender frame and quickly swallowed the moisture from her body.

She then rushed across to the hut which stood on two poles, six feet over the ground.

She got dress into leopard skin clothing and walked towards the doorway of the little hut, looking out across the swimming pool.

How quiet it was on these lazy days under the straw eaves of the small house. Before the doorway, the half-ripped fruit dangled high on the ajap tree and still, Chimp, her pet monkey, swayed from one branch to another, performing impressive scolding, and gymnastic feats because she didn't laugh and yell her approval.

Time went slowly, the eleventh-hour oppression of the hot sun was at its receding tide, its intense violence done to the yellowish soil of the clearing, and the rich tapestry of the great forest drooped breathless over its secret; for here, deep in the African Congo, was the sacred dwelling place of Abigale, the Golden Queen of the Forest and all its men.

Here no one had ever set foot, not even those who flaunted the title, Bwana and whose skin was white.

Fools perish quickly on the forbidden trails of the Congo forest and the wise knew better than to display tribal taboos.

The rain was past due, the heat overbearing in the small clearing even hours after the sun goes down. The thunder rolled like the drums of the forest, Lightning flashed across the horizon and nature waited in gasping suspense.

But no rain came, Abigale longed for it to come and bust this brooding hush, though she knew that it has to make her forest home damp and depressing, this anxious waiting for something to occur was driving her insane.

This season, a strange new feeling had beset Abigale, a feeling that was constantly growing out of her inner heart.

She could no longer accept that it was entirely because of the weather. It was linked with the young dealer who'd come up to the Quango post as surely as it was linked with his black, bearded acquaintance.

No white man had ever set eyes upon Abigale, not one who came into her province escaped her scrutiny. She enjoyed looking closely into their faces when sleep had taken off the mask of consciousness and revealed the bare soul.

She walked through their camps, like a phantom in the night. The hunter, the dealer, traveler and preacher—yes she knew all of them.

Many were wise in the ways of exile, and came and went their ways; while others came out of the forest with secret and a troubled look on their faces.

Occasionally one or two stayed too long in the forest, and then, as the Abamas said:

"He sent his heart into the dark," and built out of his lonely terror and the permit of aloneness; an obstinate habitation for his spirit. Such men were regarded as dangerous, as lethal as the mamba.

And this type of man was called the Black-Rashidi, the one with big gold rings in his ears.

He wore a wicked face, with an evil twist to the mouth even when he seem relaxed. But, the youthful one, flung out on his canvas bed, tanned torso and muscular limbs covered by mosquito netting, was not hard to look at.

He had beautiful black curls beside the white of his pillow, he had a strong masculine face softened by some dream that made him smile in his sleep. Not too tall, maybe, as tall as Menelik, leader of the Abamas, but then Menelik was a giant of a man.

Was it evil she'd seen in the face of the one, or was it the troubling thought which came to her when she thought of the other, that kept her in idleness beside this forest pool?

Abigale found it difficult to tell. The ambiguity made her temperamental and reawakened in her a hankering for the trails long accustomed to her--the trails that curled and wound strangely around the mountains, down through the shadowy forest, and in the valleys.

Chimp bounced up onto the flooring beside her and dropped to the ground. She spoke gently to him what was on her mind, and ran her hand through his black hair:

"Very soon Chimp, the rain will come. We will leave this place tomorrow and go to the cave in the mountains."

Chimp frowned and looked up at her. This is the longest they had ever stayed in this place. He sensed his mistress' unhappiness, and he felt bad.

He was uneasy and could not keep still. He swung swiftly up into the ajap tree again, and sat scolding her in his comical way.

The sun slowly disappear behind the mountains, and the clearing was overflowed by darkness. The surrounding forest was windless, yet full of hurried sounds, and the lingering song of the bush cuckoos. Shortly the drums, in the deep, consuming the quietness of the forest like the snapping of a giant telegraph, began to speak.

At this very hour all the people in the villages gave ear to the chattering of the forest.

The drums were not of identical sound, nor were their voices more alike than the voices of people. Abigale never failed to recognize a drum by its own voice. In the old, prehistoric code all of the facts of life had their idioms, all the adventures and misadventures of the day, their statements; and no leader, regardless of the white man's magic, understood the fears and hopes of the people.

No one knew then better than Abigale, The Queen of the Forest.

"Your wife gave birth to a son!" one drum announced. And someplace deep in the forest, or on the veldt, a lonely hunter stopped to build a ceremonial fire and give thanks to the forest gods.

Then from the darkness, as swift as an arrow aimed at her heart, Abigale heard her very own name, her own drum name, and joined with it was this phrase:

"Peron is dead. The Mighty Rashidi killed him. Come quickly, cross his hands on his breast!"

And then immediately after that, there was a desperate cry in the wilderness as one drum, and then another, and another, cried out an old, distressing call to mourning.

Under the instant thrust of it all, life in the clearing seemed to be detained, and Abigale's heart was as cold as ice in her chest.

Then, abruptly, she leapt to her feet, her hands clenched tight, her blue eyes blazing like fire. So, they'd dared to kill one of her people, a courageous and brave hunter.

So, this was the reason why her spirit was in distressed, her un-quiet spirit had tried to warn her.

But she'd not listened to the still small voice within her. She'd seen the evil in the face of Rashidi, yet she ignored it and did not send Menelik's warriors to drive him out. No, she'd not done that, in her heart lurked a concealed wish to speak to the youth one! Ah, but now, she wasn't deaf to the small voice. Send a message to the white men for them to beware, very soon they will meet with Abigale face to face!

She grabbed her bow and quiver that was hanging from a peg above her bed; then raced down the dappled trail to the village of the Abama's , as fast as a cloud shadow over the veldt, as light as dust. Chimp saw when she flash down the trail from his perch in the ajap tree, and screeched out his protest.

To keep off the forest trails at night was just plain monkey-sense.

At dawn Abigale stood on a rocky eminence, looking straight toward the distant mountains, a superb body that was beautiful with her hair flowing out in the hot wind from the south.

The rippling open country ran out to the foothills, and there were pools of darkness under the euphobia trees which pointed pale-jade fingers against the calm azure of the sky.

But Abigale looked upon the recognizable panorama, frowning, not deceive by its beauty.

The creeks were showing ripples of sunbaked mud across the plain, and there was the stench of rotting fish in the wind. The land was drying up under the oven-heat of the sun, and the strong wind from the desert.

All the game was drifting towards the west-- the zebra and the eland in flitting stampede to avoid the leopard and the lion slinking on their flanks. If the rain didn't come soon, it would not be good for her people who pastured and hunted their herds on this plain.

In the far distance, smoke was discharged from the huts of the Abama village to smudge the blue sky. Quickly she sped on.

The village was enclosed by a hill and strayed along the fast-drying river which looped around it like a mighty python. Abigale had been born among the Abamas, but not in this village.

All she knew of her past had come to her from the lips of old Nidi Ela, the witch-woman of the tribe.

And that was a very long time ago that it was difficult to recall what the old woman had said. But occasionally, as now when she drew near to the village, a graphic image of Nidi Ela would appear in her mind, and she would see the old woman strike the ground with drone and her staff:

"This and I--we're quite old! Very soon I will go the Black Kloof. I've words for you before I go.

Your mother and father were of the Tribe of God. Your skin is white, my little one. You, too, are of the Tribe of God, and it's not good for you to play with black kids.

I am going to inform my people to build a hut for us in the forest.

I am going to teach you my craft.

Then, when I'm no longer on this earth, you will be the people's yenda, their wise-woman, and they must obey you."

And so it'd come to pass. For a very long time she had been living in the forest, drinking of Nidi Ela's black wisdom, until she'd sucked the fountain dry.

And every day she grew more, and more beautiful and radiant in her youth under the African sunshine. More than once Nidi Ela had taken her to the village on the Day of Testing when the young men of the Abama clans assembled to demonstrate their fitness for wedlock and war.

In those competitions no man had proved himself fleeter on foot, or fatal in his purpose with the bow and the spear.

The story of wisdom and her skill was carried from one kraal to another, so that there were few village headmen who would have thought to venture upon any endeavor without having first consulted with her.

At times she wondered at Nidi Ela's unfamiliar words. Since the Abamas called all missionaries Men of the Tribe of God, she supposed that her father had been a missionary.

Beyond this she could barely think. It was foolish of her to even try, like pulling at a vine to which there was no fruit.

No one was moving on the dusty trails that crisscrossed the village. The birds held their wings fan-wise to catch the air, while the goats lay panting under the ironwood trees.

The mushroom houses, shaggy with the thickest of palm-leaf roofing, hunkered under the burden of sun, but in the palavar house there was permanent dusk.

The sudden glitter of copper decorations was there, and the glitter of spear heads.

Bright eyes set in dark faces, eccentric headdresses covered with beads, buttons and shells, the intense and tumult gestures of dispute were there also--and then complete silence when Abigale came to stand among them.

Abigale's eyes picked out Menelik, the youth leader of the Abamas. "My ears are open, Menelik," she said.

"The white men sent a runner to our village," the leader said as he got to his feet, "because they wanted to do business with us. As you already know, Abigale, we're mighty and great hunters and there's an ivory waiting under each and every man's bed in this village. It seemed good to me that we should exchange some of it for firearms. And--"

"Why did you ask for firearms?" Abigale interjected sharply.

Menelik felt uneasily and looked around him, he then took a deep breath and at length:

"Nothing can be kept secret from Abigale. We need all the firearms we can get our hands on to go against the Arab's town. Many years ago he drove our folks. He drove our brothers, the Mamas, made slaves of their young men and stole many of their women. If I think to make war against him, is it a terrible thing?"

Abigale gave him a long ice-cold stare. "Maybe," she said gently, "Menelik thinks too much of war. Maybe, to be the Leader of the Abamas is not good for him at this moment."

A low murmur ran round the group of seniors, and Menelik looked down at the ground. Not until the Forest Queen smiled on him again would his grip on the chieftainship be firm. For a moment Abigale kept him in an agony of suspense, then abruptly she smiled:
"A man should always speak his heart even though it betray his folly. I'm very pleased with your leader, since he did this without fear. But in your fathers' time the Abamas, like silly young bulls, rushed against the walls of the Arab, and their horns was broken.

The Arab would be too powerful for you, Menelik, even if you'd lots of guns. Do not consider going into war with him. Now, go on with your story."

"I sent my uncle, Peron, with two hands of teeth to the dealer's kraal," Menelik took up his story. "I did this because once Peron was on safari with Rashidi, and he knows the Swahili language that the dealers use, I sent just as many men as were needed to carry the ivory.

Truthfully, my head was sick when I did that! Rashidi would not give Peron guns. No, He deceived Peron. He offered only beads and cloth.

This made Peron very angry because he already knew that the dealer offered less for ten teeth--large teeth, I say--than a coast dealer would give for one." He stopped to catch his breath, then went on:

"Then Peron would have left the dealer's kraal, but Rashidi wouldn't let his men touch the ivory. There was a fight. The trader drove our people. Peron ran for the bush, but Rashidi fired his gun and Peron fell. Then the people rushed out and captured five of our men, and took them into their kraal.

They took Peron also. Probably, he's not alive. Without a doubt, also, the others will be killed if we go against him. Now, we ask you what we should do about this matter." He sat down, and all eyes were turned upon Abigale. She was silent for a while, then:

"Menelik, you spoke only of Rashidi. Where was the young Bwana when all this happened?"

"We do not know, Abigale." He swept his arm out and muscles rippled under his black, satin skin. "All who survived are with us now. And it is said that the young, white man wasn't there."

The smile on Abigale's face came and went fast. Merely for a second it made her dark eyes shine in the dim light. It was a fleeting glance of the real warrior woman behind the taboo that was constantly before her like a shield. Menelik saw it and, quickly guessing what had encouraged it, glowered and spoke a thought conceived by the wish:

"Maybe he's gone down the river to the shore."

Abigale shook her head slowly. "No, I doubt it very much, the drums would have revealed it," she said, and then went silent, her eyes muddled with thoughts running through her mind.

Several minutes went by without a single sound except for the heavy breathing of the old men. Then:

"The dealer must be shown that he cannot deceive and shoot our people as he wish," she said. "We will drive him."

"This is good! This is good!" All the elders approved in on voice. Except for Menelik, he seemed doubtful.

"How should we go against them, Abigale?" He asked. "They have a very strong kraal. They've lots of guns. Also, they've five of our men held in captive."

The Forest Queen smiled. "You're a man of war, Menelik, and you've nothing in your head but spears and firearms. This is what I command. You have enough ivory, also.
Rashidi wants ivory, and so you are going to build a large trek and take all the ivory there."

Menelik's jaw dropped. For a very long time he stared at her in complete bewilderment. At last he gasped out: "So, your plan is to give him the ivory in return for our captured men?"

Abigale laughed. "It's my plan," she said, "to teach him, and you, a lesson, Menelik. Follow my plan, and all will be well. Prepare yourselves to march at sunrise.

Leave your spears behind. Let no man take more than his knife. I've spoken."

"I hear, and obey," said Menelik.

At the doorway of the palavar house she turned abruptly and asked: "Do your wives still sew well, Menelik?"

"Yes, Abigale."

"Great!

I will go and speak with them now." Wearing an expression of deep puzzlement, Menelik followed her out into the sunlight.

CHAPTER TWO

*****

Tough Dealer and hunter he was, Scott Thorne felt out of his depth in this remote trading post on the Portuguese side of the Quango River.

It wasn't the loneliness, or the heat that troubled him--he was used to both. It absolutely was Lazaro Jesse who'd given him a terrible case of the jitters.

The Portuguese had a bad temper, and his patchy head, scorched by the hot sun, his long bent nose and his beady eyes, joined to give him a predatory appearance, strongly suggestive of a bald-headed eagle that as a young lad Scott had watched circling the hills in far-off Montana.

The worst of it was, before he'd left the shore two months ago he had been warned against Jesse's blind fits of rage.

And Jesse was about through as senior representative up on the Quango, as stated by the Chief Factor of the Companhia do Nayanda.

"His record isn't great," Freire had told him when he'd taken the job. "I'll be honest. Sandor Jesse hasn't asked for an assistant but I'm sending you up to him. I would like to have a better understanding of what is wrong up there, and I expect you to find out and report back to me.

And I'll give you a fear warning. Always be on your guard and look out for yourself, Sandor. Watch Jesse very carefully, he's the devil himself."

The Chief Factor had made it clear that he strongly believed Jesse was trading with the company's goods on his own account. And, surely, there was much in Jesse's talk to justify that suspicion.

From the very first day he arrived, it seem to Scott, Jesse had been giving him signals, hinting darkly at some cunning scheme he had worked out, a scheme that will make a bright young man rich in a very short time if he knew how to keep his mouth shut.

And now there was this trouble with the Abamas. Why on earth had he picked this day to go hunting? There'd be hell to pay, in the event the old Abama headman strike.

Everywhere seem to be quiet now, dozing in the late afternoon sun. A shimmering, cobalt bowl, spilling withering fire back on the red dirt of the compound. The sky was clear, Jesse was relaxing and drinking gin in an old cane chair.

"Where did you put that fellow?" Scott asked abruptly.

Jesse pushed his glass out in the direction of one of the huts that faced the bungalow across the compound. "In there," he answered, and then added coldly:

"He will die before sundown. They always do."

A muscle in Scott's jaw tightened, but he said calmly: "We're sitting on a powder keg, Sandor. I think you should send the other men back to their village before—"

"I heard you the first time!" Jesse snapped. "And I tell you again that I am in charge here. I give the orders." He touched the butt of his revolver. "If a black talks back, whip him; if he puts his hand on a weapon, shoot him.

That's my rule, and when I give orders I make no distinction between white men and black men. Remember this, Sandor, and you will not get hurt."

Scott's mouth was shaped to an oath as he turned on his heel and went into the main room of the bungalow.

He went straight to the big medicine chest which stood over against the wall from the door. From it he took out his own first aid kit. When he straightened up Jesse was standing in the doorway, his eyes narrowed to slits.

"What are you going to do with that?" he demanded.

"What I can for that poor devil you plugged," Scott told him calmly.

"Holy Saints!" Jesse's face became charged with blood. "Did you not hear me tell you to keep away from him?"

Scott put the case down on the floor with slow deliberation. He considered Jesse thoughtfully for a moment before he said: "I'm not a doctor, but I took a course in first aide at Luanda. And I'm not going to sit here and let that poor devil die just to please you."

"So!" Jesse spat on the floor, then: "Just now I told you that I give the orders here." His hand went down to his holster, and then jerked up as he started back against the wall and froze to it. "Holy Saints!" he gasped.

At the first downward movement of his hand Scott's Colt had flashed from its holster as if by magic. Its muzzle pointed skyward, and the light glinting on its bright metal was reflected by his gray eyes.

"Any cowhand where I come from could teach you gun-play, Sandor," he said quietly. "I don't know what you've got against that Abama out there, and I don't know why you blasted him. I do know that you'd better get rid of that gun. If you're packing it when I come back I'll take it to mean that you want to shoot it out."

The Colt spun on his finger, and plopped snugly back into its holster. He picked up his case and walked across the room. The bravado had been shocked out of Jesse. He kept his hands shoulder high and backed out of Scott's path.

The wounded Abama was stretched out on the dirt floor of the hut, with his face turned to the wall. Gently Scott rolled him onto his back and knelt to examine the wound.

The native was badly hurt, unconscious. At a glance Scott saw that the deltoid muscle had been torn clean across near the right shoulder joint.

The ends of the sinew had contracted, and if the man was to have the use of his right arm again the torn ends of the muscle must be pulled together expertly. It was a job beyond Scott's skill. The Abama groaned and opened his eyes as Scott probed and cleansed the wound.

Fear came into his eyes, but faded as Scott patted his shoulder and smiled. Scott made things easier for him with a little opium and, as he bandaged the wound, the native said faintly in Swahili:

"It is hard to die so far from my village, Bwana."

"You will not die," Scott told him. "I will take you downriver to the mission station. What is your name?"

"Peron, Bwana."

"You speak good Swahili, Peron. Perhaps you have traded with Bwana Jesse before?"

"Even so. Once I was his headman. I showed him the way to Kilmer, the Arab's town."

Scott started so violently that the roll of bandage fell from his hand. He let it roll across the dirt floor, and asked: "You took ivory there, Peron?"

"Oh yes, Bwana! Big teeth we took there."

With a grunt of satisfaction Scott crawled after the roll of bandage. He saw it all now. Jesse was already selling ivory to Leman bin Ali who possibly will send it down to the Congo and then to the Belgian ports without anyone noticing.

He giggled softly.

Leman bin Ali was an opportunist of the old school He should have known from the start that if there was a crooked dollar to be made in the Congo the old sinner would be reaching for it. No wonder Jesse had not wanted him to talk to Peron! At the thought his face sobered, and he said:

"Let no one know that you have told me this, Peron. You will not leave this place alive if you do." Then he thought that he'd better make sure of it, and he gave Peron a knockout dose of opium. "Rest now," he said. "I will come for you soon."

Jesse was sitting on the rail of the verandah when Scott came back. If he had a gun it was nowhere to be seen. He tugged at his beard nervously as Scott came up the steps. Scott dropped into a cane chair and, tilting it back, rolled a cigarette with aggravating slowness.

"Well?" demanded Jesse.

"He's got a good chance if he gets proper care. With your permission I'll take him down to Sao Vincent."

Sudden fear came into Jesse's eyes. "So—to the mission, eh? What did he tell you?"

Scott shrugged and said, "I doped him, and I'll have to keep him that way until he's over the shock. Besides, what could he tell me? I don't speak his dialect."

A gleam of satisfaction came into Jesse's eyes. "Nothing, Sandor—nothing!" he said with obvious relief. "I thought that perhaps you would blame me.

Well, I am to blame. You see, I am just. I have a heart, too. Take him to Sao Vincent, my friend. Yes, and tell the good fathers that I will pay for everything."

Scott's slow smile quirked the corners of his mouth. "Well, that's generous," he said. "It won't be safe to move for a couple of days, though."

"Do not delay too long, my friend. Holy Saints, I have never known the rain to hold off for so long. In another week there will be enough water in the river to float a canoe, and it may be that you will have to come back on foot."

"Well, I'll have to take that chance," said Scott, frowning. "Right now the trip would kill the poor devil."

"You know best," said Jesse. "When you are ready to go take Banja and five of my Swahilis. They know the river and will make a quick trip for you."

Scott was not particularly happy in the choice of Banja. Jesse's headman was a civilisado, and his exaggerated idea of the privileges of Portuguese citizenship sometimes pushed him into downright insolence. But he wanted to keep Jesse unsuspicious until he had Peron safe in the mission hospital, and raised no objection.

During the two days that followed two things began to worry Scott. One was the vague feeling of uneasiness that Jesse's changed attitude gave him. There was a lot more going on than his fear of his Colt behind the Portuguese's surprising affability--something he could not put his finger on.

The next was just as equally intangible, but so strong in its suggestion of brooding threat that it kept him pacing on the verandah of the bungalow a few hours.

It was the unusual quietness that had come to the forest.

Not a single sound of drum throbbed during the nights, and none of the native came in their canoe to barter fish on the bamboo float which jutted out into the wide river. The post was isolated, the natives avoiding it as if it were the center of a plague.

On the morning of the third day he stood on the verandah looking upstream. The river was falling, and from the exposed ooze that was open, baking in sunlight, came the effluvia of decay and corruption.

Beyond the very first bend of the river there was no view, just the boundless expanse of the forest, looking more grey than green, without perspective or shape, silent, foreboding. The bamboo jetty was still afloat, but doubted that it would be tomorrow. He decided to leave at sundown for Sao Vincent.

He went into the bungalow to announce his decision to Jesse, but before he could get the words out of his mouth a sudden commotion broke out in the compound. Then Banja came running to the verandah steps.

"Safari, Bwana!" he shouted at Jesse. "Big safari!"

Both white men ran out onto the verandah and saw many paddles flashing in the sun. Soon the black shapes of a dozen big dugouts could be seen moving rapidly downstream, the beat of a drum timing the rhythmical stroke of the paddles.

Strung out in a long, slanting line they came lurching toward the float. As the first canoe slid alongside three big natives leaped out of it. Four others immediately began to pass out the canoe's cargo into the hands of their fellows on the float.

In a moment a half-dozen prime tusks lay at their feet. Another canoe shot alongside, and another, and another, and the same process was repeated. Jesse's eyes bulged as the pile of coffee-brown tusks grew larger and larger.

"Holy Saints!" he cried out at last. "Not one under forty pounds!" In his excitement he slapped Scott on the back. "Sandor," he exclaimed, "all my life I have dreamed that something like this might happen to me! Ho, Banja! Open the gates! Break out a keg of rum for our guests!

Don't stand there gaping, you black scum, jump to it!" Again he slapped Scott's back. "That's the trick of it, Sandor, all there is to it! Get 'em dead drunk, treat 'em like hidalgos and they'll trade a prime tusk for a coil of copper wire."

"They'll catch up with you one of these days," Scott told him with a shake of his head.

A long file of blacks was moving up the steep trail to the gates, not all of them shouldered an ivory, but Scott counted thirty-six.

He did a little mental arithmetic, and whistled at the total. There was close to a hundred thousand dollars walking up that trail, or he didn't know a prime tusk when he saw one!

Then his attention was drawn to the last canoe to reach the float.

Four big blacks, one of them a gigantic fellow wearing the headdress of a chief, were lifting something out of it—something sewn up in a hammock of skins. With a puzzled expression he watched the four set the hammock down on the float carefully and run a stout bamboo pole through the lashings looped around it.

Then they lifted it shoulder high, and came jogging up the trail.

"What do you think they had there, Jesse?" he wondered.

But the Portuguese was out in the compound, driving his crew of Swahilis to work. The doors of the big trade shed were swung open. Soon every man was rolling out kegs, breaking open bales of cloth and stacking them on the shelves that lined three sides of the huge shed.

They moved fast under the lash of Jesse's tongue and the sting of Banja's cane.

CHAPTER THREE

*****

A s the leading files of the safari passed into the compound Jesse came back to the verandah to receive its headman.

There was none of the clamor and excitement that usually turned the post into a pandemonium upon the arrival of a caravan.

The porters quietly left their ivories in front of the house; then, as if at an unseen signal, as quietly they all trooped across the compound to form a solid phalanx before the open doors of the trade shed, and stood silently watching the busy, sweating Swahilis within.

Observing this maneuver, Scott's eyes widened in sudden alarm.

He touched Jesse's arm and said quietly:

"We've got trouble. These fellows aren't porters, they're warriors!"

But Jesse could not take his eyes from the ivory. "Nonsense!" he muttered. "There's not a spear among them, and—Holy Saints, what is this?"

He broke off pointing as Menelik and his warriors set their burden down at the foot of the verandah steps.

As if in answer to his question the Abama chief drew his knife, and threw a quick look around the compound. Then he ripped open the seam of the skin bundle, and Abigale burst from it, like a gorgeous butterfly from its chrysalis.

Bow in hand, poised to draw and shoot, she faced the two dumbfounded white men. At a nod of her golden head, Menelik bellowed out a command. The Abamas near the shed dashed forward, threw their weight against the doors and swung them shut, trapping every man the post could muster within.

Abigale's blonde beauty held Scott spellbound. Jesse was the first to recover from the shock of it all. He gasped:

"A raid! Your gun, Sandor! Holy Saints—" He started to run for the door of the bungalow, evidently with his own gun in mind.

"Hold!" said Abigale, in a clear ringing voice. At the same instant her bow twanged. The arrow plunged into the door post just ahead of Jesse, and he pulled up with his hooked nose touching the quivering shaft.

"Be still!" commanded the Forest Queen. With her eyes fixed on the young trader she notched another arrow. He appeared to be shaking the stupefaction that had taken possession. He passed his hand before his eyes, shook his head, and muttered something in a tongue she did not know.

He was almost as tall as Menelik, and his eyes were very bold when open. There was no fear in them, but something else was there—a gleam that pleased her and yet made it hard to give him stare for stare. He seemed to sense her discomfiture; for a slow smile came to his lips, and he said in Swahili:

"Lady, I have seen many strange things, but never a thing as strange as your coming—or a thing as beautiful as I see now. It cannot be that you have come to steal like a bushman."

"Why like a bushman?" she flashed at him. "Why not like a white trader? They are the great thieves. Your friend has killed one of my people, and he has taken five others. I know that you were not here when this was done, and that is well for you, Brass Eyes!"

She shifted her gaze to Rashidi, and her blue eyes snapped at him. "Are you as ready to die as you are to kill?" she asked.

He made a queer animal noise in his throat, and his fear oozed out of him like a smelly sweat.

His eyes darted frantically around the compound, but could find no way of escape. He could not speak, so great was his fear; and his eyes held the dumb pleading look of a sick dog when he turned them on his young companion. Brass Eyes spoke for him:

"Peron is not dead, Lady. This man has done evil, but he is sorry for it. Is it not the custom of these—of your people to hold a palavar when a wrong has been done to them? My friend is willing to talk, to pay whatever you ask."

Abigale regarded him steadily for a time. He was not afraid, this one, and it was only fear that made men lie.

"Where is Peron?" she demanded.

He pointed to one of the huts. And, at a nod of her head, Menelik sped across the compound to it. Not a word was spoken until he returned.

"He speaks the truth, Abigale," Menelik reported in a low voice. "Peron speaks well of the young Bwana. There is some trouble between him and the other, but Peron does not know what it is."

"Good!" said Abigale. "Seize Rashidi, and then search all the huts for guns."

Rashidi shrank back as Menelik mounted the verandah steps, and the young one looked as if he would show fight. She laughed softly, and then said: "Be still, Brass Eyes. We are too many for you, and it is no longer in my mind to kill your friend. We will talk now, you and I."

Jesse yelped as Menelik took hold of him. He struggled trying to pull away from the Abama chief's iron grasp.

"Sandor!" he appealed to Scott. "Help me—Holy Saints, you cannot let this she- devil—"

"Better go quietly, Jesse," Scott told him. "You've been asking for something like this for—"

"Speak Swahili!" Abigale told him sharply.

Then Menelik lost patience with the twisting and screaming Portuguese. He hit him once, then heaved Jesse's limp body over his shoulder like a dead buck.

He stepped aside as Abigale came up the steps and went into the bungalow.

The young one followed her in. She was conscious of his eyes. They never left her as she glided across the room and sat in one of the cane chairs. He came to a stand, looking down at her, his gaze disconcertingly warm.

"Lady," he said with his slow smile, "when I saw you first I thought that I was dreaming. Even now I am not sure that I am awake."

"Are women with white skins so strange to you?" She held his gaze as the snake holds the bird's that it will soon devour.

And suddenly she knew that she had power over this man, and yet there was a recklessness, a wildness in him that she could not help but see. Here was a spirit as strong and free as her own.

She had the power to stir him, even to control him with her smiles, but he would not tremble at her frown as Menelik did. To make this one her slave she would have to share the burden of his chains.

"Who are you?" he asked in his wonderment. "Where do you come from?"

"I am Abigale. That is enough for you, Brass Eyes."

"BRASS EYES is not my name," he told her, frowning.

"I am Rick Thorne, hunter, trader, anything so long as it keeps me on the move. Call me Scott, it will make it easier for me to believe my eyes."

"Scott—Scott," she repeated the name and smiled, then: "It is a little name to give such a big man." Then her face sobered, and she asked: "Tell me why I should not take all the trade goods here and give them to my people? Rashidi has wronged and cheated them. Would it not be just?"

"No!" he answered promptly. "It would not because the goods do not belong to Rashidi. Lazaro Jesse is his name. The goods belong to the Company I work for, and taking them will do Jesse no harm. Listen, Lady—"

"Abigale."

"Well then, Abigale. Now I will tell you about Jesse…"

She listened to all he had to say, and liked the deep, resonant tones of his voice. When he stopped talking she was silent, turning it all over in her mind. Suddenly she asked:

"This man you hunt for, he will think well of you if you send all the ivory my people brought in down the river to the coast?"

He gave her a startled look, then his slow smile came. "Truly, he would think well of me," he said. "He would think me a prince among traders."

"Good! Then I will tell Menelik to make fair trade with you. I do this because of what you will do for Peron."

"I would do it for any man," he said. "We leave at sundown, as I have said." Then his eyes became troubled, and he asked: "What about Jesse?"

"Have no fear for him. As you say, it is best to give him up to his own people for punishment. He knows nothing, and Menelik will make fair trade with him while you are downriver. Also, Menelik will watch this place until you come back. Do as you will with Jesse then. Now, I go." She rose in a swift, lithe movement and moved to the door. He sprang to intercept her.

"Where are you going?" he asked, and caught hold of her arm. "You can't walk in and out of my life like this!"

At the touch of his hand she felt her heart jump, then she stiffened and thrust him back. "Are you weary of life?" she bashed at him. "No man may touch me. If my people saw your

46

hand on me their spears would drink your blood!"

The unexpected strength behind the thrust of her arm had thrown him back several paces, and the look that came to his face was almost funny in its expression of complete astonishment.

"What are—who—what the heck—" He gulped, and gazed at her, dumbstruck. She chuckled softly, then turned and walked away, left him still staring.

Later that evening, from behind a screen of bush, she watched Scott and his men carry Peron down to the river on a mat of woven grass.

When the canoe was an amorphous blur on the yellow water, in a mood compounded of nameless yearnings and a strange feeling of emptiness, she took the trail back to her forest sanctuary.

Scott made good time downriver, arriving at Sao Vincent a little before sundown two days later. The town was typical of the Portuguese frontier—a cluster of flat-roofed, pink-and-whitewashed adobe houses, clinging to the river bank with the indefatigable forest pushing at them from behind.

The assignment of Carmelite friars was a stone house with beautiful castle walls, and cool curved corridors covered by palms.

While Peron was in the hospital, Scott talked with a fat, worldly- looking brother of the order.

"Christian charity is rare in these parts," said the monk. "You have done an act of mercy for which God will reward you, my son."

"Well," smiled Scott, "there are a lot of black marks against me up there, Father. I'll be lucky if I get a cancellation on this. And, by the way, have you ever heard any talk of a white woman—a sort of goddess—up on the Quango?"

"Oh, yes! The natives are full of such tales. But it is wise to believe in such marvels only when we see them, my son."

"And it is not always wise to talk of the marvels we see, eh, Father?"

"Not if we wish to be thought truthful, my son."

"That's how I figure it," murmured Scott. Then, "Well, I must leave tonight. It is my wish to pay for Peron's care now."

The monk chuckled. "Ah, you are a jewel. Nothing is asked, nothing is expected, but a gift is always thrice blessed," he added as Scott pressed a small bag of coins into his hand. "God go with you, my son!"

The Quango was falling rapidly now. A few miles above the town Scott, Banja and his four Swahilis were forced to abandon their heavy canoe. They continued the trek on foot, through the scented cedar forest and across the burnt veldt.

Herds of zebra thundered southward, the scent of greener pastures strong in their nostrils. The natives were leaving their villages, trekking for Sao Vincent in anticipation of famine.

Short rations forced Scott to shoot for the pot, and the heat forced him to short, night marches. A trek of no more than three marches under normal conditions dragged out to six, and it was near noon on that day when he marched into the Quango factory.

The post was deserted. The compound empty.

After the first shock of it was over, Scott soothed the fears of his jabbering Swahilis.

"There has been no fighting, Banja. Bwana Jesse must have marched downriver with the ivory."

"Doubtless he has marched with the ivory!" The headman spat on the ground. "But not down to Sao Vincent," he added with a vehemence that caused Scott to give him a sharp look. But the Swahilis were crowding around them with bulging eyes, and he only said:

"Come to the bungalow, Banja. We will talk of this."

Papers littered the floor of the main room, and the storeroom had been rifled. Jesse had taken all his small safari could carry, plus the ivory. But there were several cases of canned food left. Also a dozen muskets stood in the rack, and there was powder and shot.

Looking around, Scott wondered vaguely why Jesse hadn't set fire to the post. He supposed that it was because Jesse had wanted to get away quietly without attracting the attention of the native villages. But what had happened to the Abamas and Abigale who had said they would watch the post?

Then a crushing sense of defeat twisted his mouth awry with a grimace of self-deprecation, and drove everything else from his mind. Freire had sent him up to watch Jesse, and Jesse had walked out of Quango with a hundred thousand dollars' worth of ivory—taken it right from under his nose!

He could hear the old timers chuckling over it—"Did you hear about the fast one that dango, Jesse, pulled on young Thorne up at Quango—" No, not that!

No man could make a monkey out of Scott Thorne and get clean away. Anger so intense that it whitened his lips and made his hands shake, swept over him.

By thunder, he'd get that ivory back. He'd get it back if he had to turn the Congo forest upside down and shake it out! He swung around to face Banja.

"You know where Bwana Jesse has taken the ivory?"

Banja's insolent eyes became fixed on a square bottle of gin which stood on a table under the window. Scott poured out a brimmer and the headman swallowed it in a gulp.

"Well?" Scott prompted him.

"Bwana," Banja began, "before you came I counted the teeth. Sometimes the number that came in and the number that went downriver was not the same. But when I told Bwana Jesse about it he only cursed me for a fool and said I could not count right. Once he flogged me so I spoke of it no more. But I am not stupid, and I have eyes."

"Are they sharp enough to find the road to Kilmer, Banja?"

"I know the road, Bwana. But we are only six. What can we do against Leman bin Ali?"

"I'll think of that when I get there. All I want you to do is show me the road." He unslung his rifle and handed it to Banja. "Is this a good gun?" he asked.

"Oh yes, Bwana!" said Banja, handling the rifle lovingly.

"It is yours, if you show me the road to Kilmer. Also, I will give a musket to each of your men, and powder and shot. Will they go?"

"Oh yes! They will march with me. What else can they do?"

"At sundown then, Banja."

"At sundown, Bwana!"

CHAPTER FOUR

✳✳✳✳✳

U p in the hills, far beyond the village, Abigale paused to listen to an Abama drummer.

She frowned as the drum spoke her nadan, and then split into accurate lengths of tumult the quiet of the forest.

In less time than it would have taken to speak the words she knew what had happened to Scott Thorne, knew that he was already two marches beyond the Quango.

Her first reaction was anger, and her wrath was turned against Menelik who had dared to disobey her, who had failed to watch the post until Scott's return, as she had told him to do. Her next thought was of Scott.

Truly, he was a reckless young fool, yet splendid in his folly marching against Leman bin Ali and all his guns with only six men!

And Menelik's fault was hers. She had promised Scott that she would watch the post and his enemy.

A fool he surely was, but she could not let him march to his death because of Menelik's disobedience. It was unthinkable. She must help Scott.

But how? She could not overtake him. Another day's march would take him deep into Leman bin Ali's country. And the half-Arab understood drum-talk, and he would send out men to capture Scott. Well then, Leman bin Ali had been a thorn in the Abamas side for a long time.

Perhaps now was the time to deal with him. Surely there was a way.

She sat down on a rock to think about it and Chimp was suddenly quiet. He came to sit beside her, his chin cupped in his hands, imitating his mistress' pose—a grotesque caricature of blond beauty wrapped in thought.

It was a long time before Abigale's eyes brightened and a faint smile of satisfaction came to her lips.

There was a way, there was always a way if she thought about it long enough. But first she must punish Menelik. With feline grace she rose and spoke to Chimp:

"Fill your belly, little one. We must travel far and fast."

When the heat waves slid down to evening and the sunlight lay in broken fragments on the village trails, Abigale's call summoned Menelik from his hut. Alone in the semi-dark of the palavar house, Abigale confronted him.

"You did not obey me!" she accused him at once.

But Menelik did not look down at the ground, nor did he squirm under the cold, angry glare of her blue eyes. His face maintained an expression of impassive innocence. And presently he said:

"Do not be angry with me, Abigale. I obeyed. I watched the trader's kraal until I could stay no longer. Four days I watched, but the young Bwana did not come, and—"

"Why did you leave? Why?" the furious girl demanded.

"Because the game left the country, Abigale. Our cooking pots were empty. We are hunters. We must follow the game. Soon I must lead my people south because of this.

We cannot stay in this place. Turn your anger against the Arogi, against the witches who hold back the rain. Am I to be blamed for what they do?"

There was a long pause, and then a deep sigh of relief came from Menelik's lips as he saw the angry light in the Forest Queen's eyes slowly fade.

"You are not to be blamed," she said. And Menelik's strong, filed teeth flashed in a broad grin. "Now I will speak of another thing," she went on. "Tomorrow we march south against the Arab's town."

The grin faded from Menelik's face and his expression settled into one of utter bewilderment. Presently he gave tongue to it: "It is a thing unheard of!"

"Are you afraid, Menelik?"

"No!" roared the exasperated chief. "I do not fear the Arab, and well you know it! But when I would have gone against him with guns you called it foolish. And now you would go against him with spears. And at such a time."

"Have I said that I will go against him with spears only?"

"Truly, you did not say so. But without guns or spears the thing cannot be done."

"Do not say of the ajap tree in fruit," she told him quietly, "that it bears nothing but leaves. Did you not think the same thing when I said I would drive Rashidi? Do as I say now and all will be well."

Menelik was silent for a long time, his face set in grave lines; then: "Always the Abamas have obeyed you Abigale. It is well for us to obey. We would be nothing without you, our enemies would have eaten us up long ago. We will obey you now. But for my people I ask why we must do this thing?"

"Because Leman bin Ali is our enemy, and because I fear that he will do harm to the young Bwana who is our friend."

"Aie, aie!" rumbled Menelik. "It is as I thought. I think back to the village where we were born, Abigale.

My heart sings at the memory of the days when we played together, and learned to shoot with the bow. Aie, they were good days! I speak of them now because there is a thing that troubles my mind, and when I say what is in my mind I know that it will make you angry."

"Truly, they were good days, Menelik. I have not forgotten them. Speak and do not fear my anger."

A dubious smile changed the young chief's eyes. Then, as when a man is about to plunge into a cold, mountain stream, he took a deep breath and said, "I speak of a thing I saw in the young Bwana's eyes when he looked at you, Abigale. If we find him alive it will be a good thing for him to leave this country."

"So!" Her blue eyes kindled.

"Even so, because if he tries to take you away the Abamas will kill him. They would do so because they love you, also because of the taboo of Nidi Ela. It is strong magic.

Even stronger than you, Abigale. You could not save the young Bwana if my people thought that you would go away with him."

And, having spoken his mind like a man, Menelik braced himself, as if he expected the roof of the palavar house to fall on his head.

But the storm did not break. No one knew better than Abigale the fatal power of imagination working through superstitious fear. It was taboo that gave her the power to command.

And something more she had.

The love of these simple forest folk who, during her helpless infancy, had cherished her as one of their own. Never had she felt the sting of a blow, never an unkind rebuke.

Her hand fell lightly on Menelik's shoulder.

"You have spoken well, Menelik," she said softly. "Now I tell you: I will leave the Abamas and this forest when the leaves of the majuti trees fall."

The saying caught Menelik's fancy. He left the palavar house chuckling over it deeply, for no man ever had seen the leaves of a majuti tree fall. It was evergreen.

Scott and his small group toiled up onto the parklands of the Mamas plateau, following the dry bed of a river that stank in like a sewer in sunlight.

The country had very gentle slopes with wild and amazing broken décor—deep kloofs and stonework fluctuating with wooded hills, some thickly shaded with mimosa bush.

That night Scott's tent was pitched in a small clearing overlooking the south- curving valley of the Simla.

The dry spell had reduced even this large tributary of the Quango to a miserable thread of water, meandering through cracks in the sunbaked clay of its bed.

Shortly cooking fires flared against the black velvet of the night.

The stillness of the encircling forest was compounded of sounds often distinctly recognizable, but as for the buzzing of the cicadas, which came barking through the aisles of the trees, and gave a knife edge to the heat.

When the late meal was over Banja left his comrades and came to squat at Scott's fire. Scott watched his broad nostrils fill with snuff, his eyes narrowed with thought.

From small things Banja had let drop, Scott had drawn at the conclusion his headman knew more of Jesse's activities than he chose to tell.

Also, Scott imagined that Banja was working toward some black end of his own, or he certainly would have quit after the very first day of the tough, dry trek.

"Kilmer is one day's march from here, Bwana," Banja announced suddenly. "Its chief is a half-Arab called Leman bin Ali."

"That I know," said Scott.

"In the old days," Banja went on as if he had not heard Scott, "Leman bin Ali came into this country with a big caravan. A Zanzibari merchant sent him, but Leman did not come back with ivory, or with the merchant's goods.

No, he drove the Mamas who lived here. He killed many and made slaves of others. Then he made them build Kilmer, and he made himself chief of this country.

He has many men and many guns. I tell you this, Bwana, because, now that we are close to his town I wonder what you are going to do."

"You might well wonder," said Scott with a wry smile.

Banja chuckled. "So you have thought of nothing. I wonder, also, what you would do with the ivory if you got it back, Bwana."

"The Company would pay well, Banja."

The headman spat into the fire. "The Company would pat you on the shoulder and say, 'Good boy! Good boy!' I know the Company! Truly, they would not give you as much as we could sell it for across the border at Bampo."

Scott smiled. So that was it! Jesse had an apt pupil in Banja. And Banja needed him for something or he would have kept his plans to himself. He said: "First we must get the ivory. How are we to do that?"

Banja grinned insolently. "For half of it I will tell you that."

"You're in bad company, young feller!" Scott told himself. "One gun against five. Better take it slow and easy, shake this jasper down for all he's got." Aloud he said:

"It is agreed, Banja. For half of it."

"Good. You do well to agree, Bwana, as you will see." He leaned forward. "Listen now. When the rain comes and Jesse can get porters he will make a caravan and march for Bampo. It is five marches from Kilmer, and we—"

"We cannot ambush a caravan with six guns," Scott interposed with quick comprehension.

"True, Bwana. But there is a Mamas village nearby. They do not love Leman bin Ali. They will make a trap for the caravan if one of the Company's Bwanas tells them to do so.
Oh yes, it will be easy—" He broke off suddenly, straightened up, and stood looking from right to left.

"What is it?" asked Scott.

Banja motioned him to silence. There was a faint rustling sound which might have been taken by a careless ear for the wind passing through the grass.
But to Banja's quick ear it was something else. He was reaching for his rifle when flame spurted out of the surrounding darkness.

Banja pitched forward across the fire without a cry. Scott's Colt roared a split second after the report of the musket. He had fired at the flash of the gun, and a yelp and the sound of a body crashing through the bush told him that he had not missed.

He flung himself on the ground and rolled out of the firelight. He could see nothing, but there was the rustle of movement all around him.

Banja's men stood bathed in the light of their fire, motionless, fearing to move lest a volley be poured into them by the invisible raiders.

Lazaro Jesse's voice came harshly out of the blackness. "You are surrounded! Throw down your gun, Sandor!"

Scott threw down his gun. Dark shapes crept out of the bush, hemming him in. Jesse pushed through them into the pool of firelight. He rolled Banja's body over with his foot, and said:

"I knew this fool would follow me but I did not think you would be so stupid, Sandor. Holy Saints, what a man you would be if you were as quick with your brain as you are with your gun. Perhaps you came to shoot it out with me, eh, Sandor Cowboy?"

"All right," said Scott from between clenched teeth. "You can shoot when you damn well please, and—"

"Kill you?" Jesse shook his head. "I see no reason to kill you. No, I will take you to Kilmer. My good friend Leman bin Ali will keep you there until I am clear of this cursed country.

Then he will send you down to the coast, and you can tell that fat pig, Friere, what happened to his ivory.

A good joke on him, eh? I deeply regret that I shall not be there to see his face when you do tell him. Holy Saints!" He slapped his thigh, and laughed until the tears ran down his cheeks.

Scott wondered if it was worth risking a blast from the guns that bristled around him just to hit Jesse once.

Jesse wiped his eyes with the back of his hand. "And they sent you to watch me," he gasped.

"How such people get rich, I do not understand. Ah, but I see that all this is very painful for you, Sandor.

Forgive me for making a fool of you also. But enough." He gave a sharp order.

His Swahilis closed around Scott. His hands were bound, a rope was looped around his neck.

The order to march was given and, cursing fluently, he stumbled through the darkness on the heels of the man who tugged at the rope about his neck.

CHAPTER FIVE

*****

It was a long exhausted walk up into the Mamas country.

Every day the Abamas padded their way along the old, tribal trails. Thin, hungry troopers stretched on the sides of the long, maundering line of children, women and old men.

A lucky hunter brought in meat for his wife to roast over the fire. The game was for south.

The village along their route were left empty, a few of the gardens and huts with the dry stalks of the guinea-corn popping in the hot wind, the true forest, an abandoned clearing, a stretch of true forest again.

In the clearings the sun was a river of fire between the walls of the forest. The forest wasn't strong but it was close, the narrow way, and broken light and color beat up into their eyes, so that the children and women and the elderly were tired after a short time. The space was very slow.

There was cassava and corn to be gleaned from the neglected gardens, but such sop didn't sit well in Abama bellies. They were warriors and hunters, and jilo, the meat hunger, gnawed at their stomachs.

Far ahead of the main body Abigale, Menelik and Chimp stood on a kopji, overlooking the valley of the Selma.

"It is bad," said Menelik. "Soon there will be no water. We should follow the game to the lake, I think."

"There is water and meat in Kilmer," Abigale told him.

"There are walls and guns at Kilmer also," growled Menelik. "It cannot be that you think the Arab will open his gates to the Abama."

"He will open them," Abigale said confidently. Then suddenly the Forest Queen tensed, looking straight ahead into the sunlight which shimmered and danced before her, rendering brightness close to zero. A cluster of scavengers wheeled in perfect grace over the painted woods. A copper armband flashed in the sun as she pointed and said:

"See yonder!"

"Aie, meat!" yelled Menelik, uttering the thought uppermost in his mind.

But another idea had flitted into Abigale's mind at first sight of the scavenger birds. With an involuntary cry of mingled fear and rage she sped down the hillside, her blond hair flowing in the wind.

Chimp went bounding after her, the Abama leader in his wake. But neither could match the flitting speed of the Forest Queen. Both were soon left far behind.

At any other time Abigale would have approached the spot with extreme caution, knowing that some beast must to have driven the vultures from their obscene feast.

But in her fear for Scott, in her anxiety to get rid of it, or to know the worst, Abigale forgot caution and burst unexpectedly into the clearing.

Abigale got a glance of the leopard bent over what was left of Banja's body, the beast spotted her and then, growling fury came plunging at her.

But the Forest Queen had an incredible swiftness and the wisdom of man, with a mind as clear and swift as a mountain stream. She knew no fear of beast or man.

Unlike the hunted creatures of the forest whose survival is dependent upon the split-second response to the impulse of flight, Abigale didn't swerve in her step but launched herself in a dive under the leopard's white belly.

The Hugh beast went down with one paw as it flashed over her.

The leopard's sharp claws went through her hair, and her arrows was ripped from her right shoulder.

The beast spring carried it half way on the other side of the clearing and, as its forepaws touched the ground, she sprang to her feet as quick as possible and turned to face it.

The confused beast crouched, tail lashing rapidly on the ground, its eyes fixed on her in an unwinking glare. The Forest Queen leopard skin was torn from her shoulder.

Her flesh had been grazed by the furious beast, and a thin trickle of blood ran down her exposed right breast. Abigale's bow was in her hand, but her quiver lay on the ground out of reach on the other side of the clearing. She dared not move, or take her eyes off the half-starved creature which, flat on its belly, was now edging toward her, inch by inch.

Abigale's hand slid slowly down to her knife, the beast's thin flanks quivered, as a snarl exposed its teeth as it position itself to spring. And just then Chimp came running into the clearing.

He came in behind the leopard, saw it, and let out an almost human scream, and then leaped for the closest tree.

Startled by the cry the leopard whirled around to confront the new foe.

In that instant, in one fluid motion the Forest Queen pounced on her quiver.

The beast sensed, rather than saw, the movement.

As quick as a flash it turned, a tawny blur in a swirl of dust and dry leaves, and sprang.

Abigale's bow twanged just as it left the ground.

She leaped aside as the big cat twisted in the air, then fell on its back, rolling over and over, snarling and biting at the arrow driven into its chest.

Then Menelik came panting into the clearing and a thrust from his leaf-bladed spear put a swift end to the beast's struggle.

When he looked around Abigale was moving up wind from the grisly remains of Banja's body, the beauty of her face marred by a grimace of disgust.

"Enough is left," she said, "to tell that his skin was black."

"Many men camped here," Menelik observed, looking over the ground. "The spoor is not cold, see!" He squatted, pointing to boot-prints on a patch of sandy soil.

"Two white men and many black fellows."

They followed the spoor until Abigale was satisfied that it would lead them to Kilmer; then she said:

"I go on. You go back to your people. Tell your warriors that Abigale says that there is meat for them at Kilmer."

Menelik rubbed his wooly head.

He was a warrior, and he was no man's fool, but for the life of him he could not see how his spearmen could break into Kilmer, and his puzzlement was profound. But what Abigale said could not be doubted.

Though he had played with her as a child, and though, outwardly, she appeared to be as other women, he had never doubted that she was something more than mortal, and possessed of powers quite beyond his comprehension. There was conviction and awe in his face when he said:

"I think that I will see a great magic at Kilmer."

Death and famine surrounded Kilmer. The fatal infectious disease of the cattle had come in the wake of the protracted drought, and on the plains vultures satisfied themselves on the remains of dead cows, spreading their wings as they reached their heads into the fetid mass, their breast feathers and wing tips greasy with fat.

But within the mud-walled town there was plenty. Its stiff thatched-roofed storage tower were full of grain, and a subterranean stream bubbled into its wells, and fed the fountain in the secluded gardens of Leman bin Ali's house.

Like most indigenous towns in Africa, all
which seemed to possess the Zulu kraal, with
its boma of thorn-bush as impassable as a
barbed wire entanglement, for their prototype.
Kilmer had two gates, one facing the other at
opposite ends of a wide, central road.

The walls enclosed an area of around five
acres, and into this space was packed, with a
large number of adobe houses with a labyrinth
of narrow lanes twisting among them.

Leman bin Ali's house overlooked the main
road, and its high-walled garden, with its green
grass, pond and fountain, jasmine and heavy-
scented hibiscus, was like an oasis in a desert of
fragrances that made Scott tremble whenever
he set foot outside the arched gate which gave
onto the dusty road.

He was allowed the freedom of the town.
Famine was his gaoler, and it was the gaoler of
Lazaro Jesse as well; for until the rain came the
long trek on the other side of the border to
Bampo was an impossible endeavor. Scott had
been given a room in Leman bin Ali's house,
and frequently he took his meals with the
venerable half-Arab who looked more like a
saint than the old rogue he undoubtedly was.

After his fashion, Ali was a god-fearing man,
stern in his observance of the letter, if not spirit,
of the precepts set forth in the Koran; the

spotless, white robe and his long white beard and the austerity he influenced were so strongly suggestive of the Biblical patriarch that Scott doubted that it was completely unconscious.

He was a generous and courteous host, and that made it simple to forget his cruelties and crimes. As the days wore on and still the rain did not come, Jesse fumed and fretted.

Scott avoided him; for whenever they met the Portuguese never failed to jibe at him, to remind him that soon he must go back to the coast and tell Freire how Lazaro Jesse had so cleverly tricked him out of a small fortune in ivory.

The whereabouts of the ivory had puzzled Scott from the first day of his arrival in Kilmer. There was no building in the town large enough to hold it.

He knew that it had long been the custom of native chiefs to bury their hoards to protect them from the rapacity of well-armed raiders; and, finally, he came to the conclusion that the ivory must be cached somewhere out in the hills surrounding the town.

Toward sundown on the fifth day of his stay at Kilmer a tribe of natives swarmed down from the hills onto the plain. From the flat roof of Leman bin Ali's house Scott watched them pour out of a narrow gap in the hills and debouch onto the veldt to cut a black swath through the tall, feathery spear-grass.

Jesse stood beside Leman bin Ali, who had an old, brass telescope clamped to one eye. Suddenly the Arab exclaimed:

"Merciful Allah! It is that daughter of Shaitan, Abigale."

"Abigale! Surely you are mistaken, my friend!" said Jesse. "What would she want of us? Not the ivory. The trade was fair."

Leman bin Ali's eyes slanted in Scott's direction as he handed the telescope to Jesse. "Wallai," he said, "you are a great fool if you cannot guess what she has come for!"

"Holy Saints, who would have thought of that!" muttered Jesse in his beard; then: "They have no guns, a volley will drive them off."

"No!" said the Arab sharply.
"If they do not attack, we do no shooting. It may be that she wants only our young friend here. By Allah, if that be all, she can have him! I want no trouble with that she-devil. See, they make camp."

He turned, shouting for one of his slaves. A Mamas boy answered his call, and Leman said:

"Go tell Ahmed to double all guards. Let him report to me when it is done."

To Jesse he said: "Those goat-skin water bags you see on the poles will soon be empty. We will know what she wants before long and, Allah willing, she will be gone in the morning."

Out in the Abama camp Abigale called Menelik to her fire.

"There is much to do before the sun sets," she told him, and then swept out her arm in a gesture that took in the surrounding hills. "Somewhere out there the Arab has hidden his ivory. Let all the people, even the women, if need be, go out into the hills to look for it."

"What good is ivory?" growled Menelik. "We cannot eat it." Then his face brightened and his deep laugh rumbled up from the pit of his stomach.

"Ho, ho!" he said.

"I think I see what Abigale is in your mind now. You will make the Arab trade meat for his own ivory! Ho, that is good!"

"Perchance he will trade his town for it, Menelik."

The chief's laughter ended in a grunt of incredulity. "He is not so big a fool, Abigale."

"We will see," the Forest Queen told him with a smile.

"When you find the ivory do not bring it into camp. Leave it where you find it. Now there is another thing. I go into the town tonight. When it is dark you will take your warriors close to the gate yonder. Let them make much noise so that the Arab will think that you are about to attack him."

Menelik looked across the plain to the high walls of the town and the thatched- roofed watchtowers standing on them. He shook his head.

All this talk of trading towns for ivory was very bewildering, and he refused to perplex himself with it any further. Silent, and wooden-faced, he went to organize the search for the ivory.

Soon the Abamas were leaving the camp in small groups to scour the hills. Abigale remained in the camp, watching the town.

Presently, two figures came to stand on the roof of Leman bin Ali's house, and the sun flashed on the brass of the tube one held to his eyes. She watched them, a faint smile on her lips.

The Arab, she knew, would guess what her people were looking for; and Rashidi would fume and sweat, because he was a man who could not control his passions.

He would want to rush out and attack the Abamas. But not Leman bin Ali. He was cautious, and he would wait until he knew the result of the search.

A woman brought her a pot of bangu, a mess of native corn and greens.

She accepted it gratefully, ate, and then slept until the noise of the Abama hunters returning to camp aroused her. The sun was down, and the shadow of the western hills was reaching across the veldt, like a black, open hand with six long fingers.

The two figures had returned to the roof of the house to watch the incoming search parties. Menelik's face was sour when he came to report:

"The Arab is a fox, and he does not hide everything in one hole. We have found some teeth. We left them where we found them, as you told us to do."

"How many, Menelik?"

"Only two hands, Abigale. But they are big teeth," he added defensively.

"It is enough. You have done well. Now, rest your warriors until the middle of the night."

There was a bright moon that night, and it made a ghost town of Kilmer. Starving jackals, driven from the carrion stinking on the plain, howled dismally on the fringe of the bush, and occasionally a dog within the town yelped a half-hearted answer to the challenge of the veldt.

When the moon was overhead, flooding the plain with the abundance of its light, Menelik and his warriors left the camp.

CHAPTER SIX

*****

Amid a great ostentation of horns and firearms they advanced across the open space, in clear view of the guards in the watchtowers.

A gun flashed twice, and the sleeping town woke up to the deep, booming alarm of a large drum. Soon many guns were snapping on the walls.

Until bullets started to whistle all around them, the Abamas continued their noisy advance upon the west gate; and then, at a shout from Menelik, they fanned out, and sank into the sea of grass.

And where there had been tumult and yelling and the flash of moonlight on spears a moment before, there was nothing to be seen now, and no sound but the rustle of movement through the tall grass.

Meanwhile, Chimp and Abigale crouched on the other side of the town in a dark place.

The shadow was cast by one of the watchtowers.

Its wooden platform, supported by angle-beams buried into the adobe, overhung the wall.

A bright rectangle of moonlight showed between the breast and the peaked roof- high fence of bamboo which enclosed the square space within.

The shape of the guards head and shoulders showed black against the sky.

A surprising blast of musketry drew the man's attention to the west gate, his back turned to Abigale. Quickly she darted forwards to within twenty paces of the wall.

There she stood for a moment, poised with drawn bow-string touching her ear. At the sharp vibrating sound of the cord winged risk sped true to her target.

The sharp, pointed arrow pierced the arm of the guard, and the impact sent him falling against the bamboo railing, knocking him out.

Under the platform Abigale uncoiled a long length of woven-grass rope and tied it around Chimp's waist.

"Up, little one!" she command, patting the wall with her hand.

There were cracks in the sunbaked adobe, but it was a hard climb even for a monkey, and Chimp nearly fell twice before he grasped and swung from one of the angle beams under the platform.

Holding one end of the rope, Abigale quickly ran to the other side of the beam, and patted the wall again, calling Chimp down.

Chimp started to come down the same way as he had gone up, but a sharp word from below stopped him.

He swung back onto the beam and jumped up and down, scolding Abigale. He was very angry. The night was full of loud and terrifying noises.

He was in no mood to play this silly game and felt safer where he was. But when he saw his mistress turn as if to go he came down in a hurry and bounded after her.

He was a very surprised and frightened monkey when the rope, which he had unwittingly looped over the beam, suddenly tightened and jerked him from his feet.

"Good, little one! Good!"

Abigale petted and soothed him as she untied the rope.

"Go now!" she hissed.

And just then a volley of gunfire crashed on the walls and Chimp went like a black streak through the grass.

A moment later the Forest Queen swung her long, shapely legs over the rail of the platform. A ladder, a tree trunk with slats bound across it, made easy her descent into the town.

It was in the dead of that night that Scott woke up with the report of a musket singing in his ears. By the time he had dressed and made his way through the garden and outside onto the central road, disaster was on the loose in Kilmer.

As Scott emerged from the arched gate a group of half-nude Swahilis rushed by, shouting like fiends. Others came running with muskets in their hands from the nearby huts as a ragged volley crashed out on the wall close to the west gate, the screams of their women grew to a shrill crescendo.

With his back flat against the wall of Leman bin Ali's garden, every man in the town with the capacity of bearing arms rushing towards the west gate, Scott's mind leapt to the obvious conclusion.

The Abamas were attacking in full force. His first thought was of escape and, embracing the wall's shadow, he began to move against the tide, heading for the east gate of the town.

At the back of his mind there was the dumb idea that if he could just get away from the town the attackers might help him to carry out the plan Banja had proposed.

But escaping was the most important thing at the moment--to get away from the nagging sense of defeat and Jesse's mockery that kept flicking at his high spirit like the lash of a vorslaag.

Darkness closed all the lanes which opened onto the main road.

The firing on the walls had slackened, and only the occasional flash of a gun tore a path under the starlit sky.

The defenders had evidently gotten to their posts in time to beat back the first onslaught.

And now silence, breathless, expectant settled on the town.

He was crossing the black opening of one of the lanes when he heard a hiss, and then his name spoken softly.

"Abigale!" He turned quickly and saw her shadowy outline against the wall of a hut.

Abigale beckoned to him, and he stepped into the shadows, and stood very close to her. His eyes were very bright and he asked in a husky voice:

"You came to help me?"

"I have come to settle an old quarrel with Leman bin Ali," she told him coldly. "He has killed many of my people and made slaves of others. It may be that we can help each other."

"I see," he said. But the disappointed look that brought a slight frown to his face told her that he saw nothing and understood less. She smiled inwardly and said:

"The attack is a trick to keep the fools looking the other way while we leave this place. If you want to go we must go quickly. You will have to run fast. Even so, a bullet may find you."

"I'll take that chance," he said. Then he pointed to the east gate. "There is a small door in the big gate. It is the easiest way out if I can creep up on the guard."

She smiled in the darkness. He was more used to giving orders than to take them. She said: "We go by the same way as I came. Come!" And she turned and ran swiftly down the lane.

Straight to the watchtower she led him and went up the ladder in a quick dash that made Scott stare for a moment. As he heaved himself up onto the platform the Swahilis on the far wall were shouting taunts at the Abamas, calling them women because they would not show themselves. Out on the plain the Abama camp fires winked.

Scott went to the rail of the platform and looked down. Abigale saw his puzzlement and there was faint mockery in her soft laugh.

"Sometimes I follow where a monkey leads," she told him. He gave her an odd, startled look.

Then he saw the stunned guard with the arrow through his arm. Abigale swung from the platform at arm's length, caught the dangling rope with her feet, and quickly slid to the ground. Scott was very nimble, and soon dropped lightly to the ground beside her.

"Run for the fires!" she told him.

"You first," said he.

She looked at him closely. Was he afraid? No, there was not a shadow of fear to dim the brightness of his eyes, now shining with excitement. And suddenly she knew what was in his mind.

He wanted to shield her with his body, to protect Abigale, Queen of the Forest! Was there no end to his folly? Did he think she was like one of the pale-faced coast women, a ninny to be petted and pampered by men? Truly he had much to learn.

But now was not the time to teach him. Without another word she sprang forward and went flashing across the open space from which the grass had been cleared for more than a hundred yards.

Again Scott stood staring for a moment, then with a muttered prayer, he started to run. There was a shot.

A bullet plucked the dirt close to his flying feet.

With a thrill of fear he realized that his white topee and shirt must show like a flare against the black of the ground.

Hot lead was sizzling about his ears as he plunged into the grass and, panting for breath, dropped to all fours. He crawled the rest of the way into the Abama camp. Abigale was waiting for him beside one of the fires.

Standing there straight and tall, with the firelight highlighting the bronzed perfection of her body, she looked like a goddess indeed. Several native women were grouped about her, naked but for a few tufts of grass. At Scott's approach they withdrew.

"Lady, you are swifter than the wind," he said.

She gave him an enigmatic smile, but did not speak. He tried to interest himself in the contents of a pot bubbling on the fire. But his mind was not on food. Always his eyes came back to her.

She found herself wishing that she had not told the other women to leave the fire. She moved back into the shadows. There was no telling what his youthful folly might prompt him to do next.

But soon Menelik and his warriors came straggling back from the sham attack. Hungry looking warriors they still were, armed with leaf-bladed spears and painted shields. Some had never seen a white man before, and came to point and stare at Scott. Then a drum began to throb, and the bystanders were drawn away to join in the dancing.

"I know you, Bwana," Menelik greeted Scott in his deep basso.

"I know you, Chief," Scott returned. "It is in my heart to hope that none of your warriors fell in the fight."

The chieftain chuckled. "There was no fight, Bwana. Those Swahili dogs made much noise with their guns, but not a bullet touched us." Then he looked at Abigale and added: "Perchance, tomorrow it will be different. Tell me, Abigale, do we play at war tomorrow, or do we drive them?"

"We drive them," she answered, and glanced up at the sky, now gray with the false dawn. "Rest now, Menelik. You, Scott, must come with me."

They left the camp and moved swiftly through the grass. It was light when they climbed a wooded hill and looked down on the west gate of the town. Vast banks of clouds, red-bellied with the first rays of the sun, hid the peaks of the distant mountains, and rolled northward on the wings of a freshening wind.

It was the first real hope of rain, and the freshness of the breeze bathed them, wiping out memories of heat, hunger and fatigue.

Abigale stood beside Scott, her breasts rising and falling as she drank deeply of the freshness of the morning. She said:

"You must help me now, because I do not think that Menelik would understand what is in my mind." She pointed to the gap in the hills, "Look well at the country before you."

They stood upon a trail that led down to the west gate. Scott's eyes followed the path through the town and across the veldt to where it entered the gap in the hills. There it joined the old caravan road to Bampo, and appeared again like a red welt on the shoulder of a low hill to the northeast of the town, and then it dropped out of sight into a densely wooded kloof.

Again Abigale directed his attention to the narrow gap. "I will give you twenty men," she said. "They will carry the ivory we found across that gap. You must make them march slowly, slowly, so that the first man will have time to run back through the bush and come out onto the road again before the last man has crossed the gap. Then—"

A sharp exclamation from Scott interrupted her. And he said something in his own tongue, but she saw the light of understanding come into his eyes. She went on:

"Leman bin Ali will think that we have found all his ivory. He will think that you are marching to Bampo with it, and he will send out his men to attack you.
Then Menelik and his warriors, who will be hidden near this spot, will rush down and break into the town.

Again Scott studied the landscape carefully, checking its features against his memory of the scene as he had seen it from the roof of Leman bin Ali's house.

His level was above that of the flat roof; yet, through the gap in the hills, he could see only that section of the Bampo road which arched over the low hill.

From the roof of Ali's house even less of it could be seen. It was a perfect setup for what Abigale had in mind. He said:

"It is like dragging a buck to catch a lion."

"Truly," she said, and then added with a faint smile: "Now you see why I had to bring you out of the town."

His awestruck expression somehow reminded her of Menelik, and did not please her at all. Then his slow smile came and went as he said:

"And a monk, a holy man, told me not to believe in miracles."

"There is no miracle," she told him with a frown.

"Men reach for what they want. In this country it is ivory they want most of all, so the Arab will reach out to grasp his ivory.

Elsewhere it may be different, I cannot tell."
And with that she led the way back to camp.

CHAPTER SEVEN

*****

On the following morning Abigale watched the dawn break over the eastern hills.

The Abamas had hidden their women and kids in a wooded valley far from town and had broken camp for the night. Scott was with his porters on the Bampo road, awaiting the sun to come from the sky.

In the bush which bordered the trail, behind Abigale, crouched Menelik and his warriors, looking down upon the sleeping town with famished eyes.

Abigale's focus became fixed on the opening in the hills, as the sun came to stand on the hills like a Hugh copper disk on edge.

Suddenly metal caught the sun's ray; and then figures, black against the red sky, appeared on the road.

Scott was leading his men with the ivory over the arch of the street.

A gap appeared in the slowly moving line of connected, black dots, and Abigale's heartbeat quickened with alarm. But shortly other dots appeared behind them.

It seems as if a Hugh caravan was moving off in the same direction of Bampo. The Abamas behind Abigale pointed and uttered soft exclamations of wonderment.

Truly, their mateyenda was possessed of powers beyond all other magicians.

"Behold!" they murmured.

"She sent only two men into the hills, and now they're as many as the stars!

It's a remarkable magic!"

Then the silence of the morning was shattered by the report of a musket. After a time two men appeared on the roof of Leman bin Ali's house. The white of Leman's robes and of Jesse's topee flared against the burned, brown of the hills.

Their movements were quick and in a moment they were gone.

Abigale grinned.

The buck was dragging, and the lion had the wind of it. Then drums started to throb in many-tongued panic. As their pressing, incessant clamor went echoing and re-echoing among the hills, she saw many white-robed Swahilis massing on the central road of the town.

Then a great cry went up as the eastern gate was thrown open, and they went streaming out across the veldt, with Jesse and Leman bin Ali in the van. Straight as an arrow the column headed for the gap in the hills.

Menelik hit against the trunk of the majuti tree, which his men had felled and trimmed, looked at his warriors, with the butt of his spear, grim visaged and impatient to swoop down on the defended town which was now weak.

"Ho, my children!

Do you smell the flesh pots of Kilmer?" his deep voice roared.

A low growl answered him and a dozen men jumped forward to lift the log shoulder high. Abigale waited until Leman's column entered the gap and vanished from sight.

Then with the Abama war-cry on her lips she sprang forward. The Abamas echoed the cry, and went charging down the slope on the heels of the Forest Queen.

Like a black wave they swept across the veldt, and the noise of their going through the tall, dry grass was like a strong wind in the forest.

A few muskets flashed as they neared the gate.

Bullets slapped into their close-packed ranks.

Several warriors fell but nothing could stop the meat-hungry Abamas. They swept on to mass before the gate. More men fell as the log was driven against the split-log barrier.

A log splintered, then another. The gate burst open under the sheer weight of their numbers as, at a shout from Abigale, they hurled themselves against it.

The few Swahilis left behind made a stand on the road. A volley was poured into the Abamas as they surged over the debris of the gate. They wavered, but Menelik's bull-like roars rallied them; and they charged, and swept over the Swahilis before they could reload their guns and discharge another volley.

After a few minutes of sharp hand to hand fighting those of the Swahilis who had not been speared in the first onrush threw down their muskets—and Abigale was mistress of Kilmer.

And it was well for the Swahilis that Menelik was not their conqueror for he was lusting to wreck bloody vengeance on the hated slavers, and it took all of Abigale's power and prestige to prevent a general massacre.

Meanwhile, at the first alarm, Scott and his little band had taken to the bush, and were now circling around the town to lead the Abama women and children to the safety of its walls.

Leman bin Ali and his column had advanced several miles along the Bampo road in hot pursuit of the elusive caravan which seemed to have melted into the dust before his eyes.

Even at the sound of gunfire he did not grasp immediately what had happened.

And when he did turn back, and again looked upon his stronghold, it was to see Scott and the Abama women and children streaming into the town through the western gate.

"Merciful Allah!" he gasped.

"That daughter of Shaitan—may she burn in hell!"

And then he was seized by a paroxysm of rage that left him in a state of collapse before it was spent.

AT sundown Leman bin Ali encamped on the plain within gunshot of the town's walls. And then began a siege which, if not unique in the annals of warfare, was a strange and rare inversion of classical examples—for while the besieged gorged themselves on the biltong in the town's storerooms and drank of clear fountains, the besiegers starved and thirsted on the sun-scorched veldt.

Leman bin Ali had the guns, but not enough powder and shot to risk an assault upon the town and Abigale did not have the man-power to risk a pitched battle on the plain. And it was not necessary that she should, since it was not in the nature of things that the siege could last long.

Calmly she awaited Leman bin Ali's inevitable submission to her will. In the Arab's garden she lay, full length on her belly in a patch of moonlight.

Outside of the enclosing walls the night was filled with the rumble of drums and the victory chant of the Abamas. She appeared to be asleep, and no sleeping forest cat could have been more still. Her hair fell in shimmering waves over her shoulders and face, but through the golden veil she was watching Scott who sat on a stone slab near the pool where the fountain gurgled and the lotus shone with the lustre of pearls in the moonlight.

The Forest Queen's eyebrows were drawn together by a frown. Something had changed Scott's attitude toward her.

Ever since the attack on the town he had been strangely silent, and he did not look at her as he had been wont to do. Even now, when he might feast his eyes in secret, he was not looking at her, but kept his eyes steadfastly fixed on the stars.

His aloofness was like the prick of a knife point. Her brain told her that there was an unspoken reproach behind it, but her woman's heart whispered that it might be something else, and became strangely tumultous at the thought.

Impulsively, she decided to put both mind and heart at rest, and got to her feet in a swift, lithe movement.

He rose from his seat as she came swaying toward him. She smiled and asked softly:

"Why are you angry with me, Scott?"

He looked surprised and answered quickly, "I am not angry, Abigale."

"Then why do you not look at me?"

The slow smile came to his lips, and he clasped his hands behind his back. "You should know without asking, Abigale. Did you not say that men reach for what they want?"

She smiled.
No, she had not lost her power over him.
It was very strong now, the gleam in his eyes and his tightly compressed lips told her that.
She felt his power too, wondered how strong it was, and her heart seemed to jump into her throat and take her breath with its wild beating. Suddenly she was conscious only of his nearness, and the primitive paeon of the drums pounding in her blood. As in a dream she heard herself say:

"So! But you keep your hands behind your back, Brass Eyes. Is that to say that you do not want me?"

She saw the startled look come into his eyes, and then his arms were about her, his kiss hot on her lips. For a moment she clung to him, forgetful of all else.

Then suddenly it flashed into her mind that this man's power to stir her was as great as her own to stir him.

In sudden alarm she stiffened in his arms and tried to push him off. But he only tightened his grip about her waist, and his arms were strong, crushing her to him.

She felt the will to resist slipping from her; and, half in anger, half in terror, she snatched her knife from her belt and drove the point into the fleshy part of his forearm.

With a startled cry he released her. She jumped back and stood glaring at him.

He was very angry, so angry that he could not speak for a moment. Then he said in a low, tense voice:

"You, you witch! You asked for that, and I'll tame you if it's the last thing I do on earth!"

"Stand back from me!" she warned.

For a long moment they stood glaring at each other. Gradually his anger died. He pulled a rag from his pocket and bound it around his forearm.

"I am sorry for that," she told him. "But you would not let me go."

He looked down at the spreading, red stain on the rag, shook his head and said: "In a forest garden I plucked a flower and a thorn drew my blood. That's an old Swahili saying."

"Do not try to pluck another," she told him. "Abama spears are sharper than thorns. Leave this country soon."

He looked at her steadily, his eyes very bright. "I'll leave," he said. "But I'll be gone just as long as it takes me to get that damned ivory down to the coast. Then I'll come back for you, Abigale."

She tossed her golden head. "Truly there is no end to your folly!" she said. "And I tell you now, as I told Menelik, that I will mate with you, or any man, when the leaves of the majuti trees fall. That is my own saying."

"And I've heard others say much the same thing," said he.

"Others? What others—who—" She checked herself as she saw the slow smile come to his lips. Furious with herself she turned away.

"I'll tell you about them, my girl," Scott muttered as she passed swiftly from sight under the arched doorway to the garden. "Someday when we're nice and cozy—and you haven't got that knife."

A little before noon on the second day of the siege Scott was called to the roof of Leman bin Ali's house, Abigale was there looking out across the plain. She pointed and Scott saw the Arab and Jesse advancing to the gate. They carried a white rag on a pole.

"We go to meet them," Abigale told him coldly.

She led the way down. Scott ran to his room and snatched up his gun-belt, and hurried after Abigale, buckling the belt about his waist as he went.

Together they passed out of the gate, and came to a halt about fifty paces from it, and waited for Jesse and the Arab to come up to them. The sun in its full meridian vigor beat down on the plain. Distant objects were blurred by the heat waves, so that the hill tops seemed to be disconnected from their bases and to hang trembling in space.

Leman bin Ali's bearing was dignified, his expression calm. Jesse smiled, but the suppressed anger in his eyes was as hot as the ground under Abigale's feet. He was the first to speak. He addressed himself to Scott:

"It is a clever trick that you have turned, Sandor. I made a joke of your wits but I am not laughing now."

"I never had what it takes to pull anything like that," Scott told him with a grin. "I'm just lucky enough to be on the right side of the fence."

Leman bin Ali was silent, pulling at his beard, and regarding Abigale with black, intelligent eyes.

"We are reasonable men, Leman and I," Jesse went on. "We offer twenty fraslas of ivory, and safe conduct to the coast."

"The ivory is not yours to give," Abigale told him coldly. "And Scott will leave this country when he is ready. Doubtless he will take you with him to the coast where your own people will punish you."

"Holy Saints, the cock is silent while the hen cackles!" Jesse exclaimed with a malicious grin.

"Be silent!" Leman's voice cut in sharply. "Abigale, I am not a fool like this one. I know when I am beaten. What is your will?"

"You will free your slaves. You will give up the ivory this man stole, and you will give up your guns so that you can raid no more villages."

"Wallai!" exclaimed the Arab, and lifted his eyes to heaven. "To the first two conditions I agree. To the last I cannot agree. I cannot leave my people unarmed among savages. Do what you will with me, but in the name of Allah I ask mercy for the women and children who call me chief."

Scott touched Abigale's arm and whispered a few words. She nodded her head and said aloud: "I will do as you ask, Scott, to show that there is no anger in my heart now." Then to

Leman she said: "My friend says that if you swear on your sacred book you will keep your word. Swear that you will not raid another kraal, and you may keep your guns."

Again Leman bin Ali lifted his eyes to heaven and spread wide his arms. "Allah is all-wise, all-knowing!" he intoned piously. "In sha Allah! I will swear on the Koran, Abigale."

"Then let it be so," said Abigale coolly. "Menelik's warriors will stay in the town until Scott has made two marches to the coast, then we will go in peace. Food and water will be sent out to your camp. I have spoken."

Just as she turned to go Jesse dodged behind the Arab, his teeth bared by a snarl of rage and hate.

Out of the tail of his eyes Scott saw his hand flash down to his gun butt. He whirled around, and the roar of his Colt blended with the report of Jesse's big revolver.

The Portuguese staggered, clutched at Leman's robe, and dragged the old man down as he fell.

"Allah be praised!" gasped Leman as Scott helped him to his feet. "Your bullet might have struck me, did he not know his own!"

He looked down at Jesse. "Dog of a Nazarani. Fool." He lifted his foot to kick the body but Abigale's voice stopped him.

"Speak softly of the dead!" said she.

"The peace of Allah be with him, and with you, Abigale!" Leman bin Ali said hastily. "And may the withering hand of old age never touch thy beauty." To which, under his breath, Scott added a fervent, "Amen!"

At last the rain came, and out of Kilmer Scott marched on the following day. From the roof of Leman bin Ali's house Abigale watched until his caravan vanished into the rain-mist that now hung over the Bampo road. Then she walked slowly down to the garden.

Again the same odd feeling of emptiness assailed her. His parting words had been: "Until we meet again!" And truly, he was fool enough to dare anything.

Absently, she pulled a flower from a bush as she walked toward the fountain, and began with a sharp intake of breath as a thorn pricked her finger.

Smiling faintly, she drew out the thorn, and watched a drop of blood ooze from the tiny wound. At a faint sound Abigale looked around.

Menelik had come to stand guard over her.

Close to the gateway he leaned on his spear, his dark face impassive, and his mysterious eyes watchful.

The Forest Queen's hand tightened on the flower she held in her hand. Her lips parted by a tremulous sigh, and she tossed the crushed flower into the pond.

Platinum House

By Stacey Hunter
Dangerous Grounds

******

Todd Marshall moved through the dense forest, taking a short-cut to the wide river which only few white hunters would have dared. He'd located a game trail that most eyes would have missed--it was just a location where the forest was a little tangled.

A huge Tawani black of his safari moved ahead of him chopping the way clear using a bush knife. About twenty five porters trailed along behind. About twelve of them carried a tusk apiece ivory.

Print Edition
ISBN-13: 978-1-68096-015-0

Platinum House
Publishing

By Stacey Hunter
Battle For The Forest

Abigale lay still on the bed of green grasses, her hands clutched behind her beautiful blond head. She was touched by a gentle wind blowing from the south through the wide open door of the tree house, whispered of a forest long awake and very busy.

But this morning the noises from the forest held no interest for Abigale. A feeling of loneliness and sadness had gripped her from the moment she woke up.

In nearby tree tops her pet monkey, Chimp, had left his noisy pursuits since sunrise to peer anxiously in the doorway in a mistress who'd lie on such a day that was so wonderful.

Print Edition
ISBN-13: 978-1-68096-009-9

Platinum House

By Stacey Hunter
Slayer's Den

Violent and unwavering was the Forest's allegiance to the wing-footed goddess—all but Galagi Yamo, famous shaker of the earth, the ancient Kalundas, who surrender to no law but his insidious juju.

******

Abigale quickly dropped from the branches of an enormous, spreading baobab and started to climb the rocky krantz, jumping lightly from rock to rock.

She was so skilled and well balanced that her slender body seemed to move, without particularized motion; and she flow with incredible swiftness in whatever direction her energy suggested, her beautiful bronzed limbs flashing in the sunlight, her golden hair flowing behind.

Print Edition
ISBN-13: 978-1-68096-011-2

Touch of Death